Deadline for McGurk

A McGurk Mystery

Also by E. W. Hildick

E. W. Hildick

Deadline for McGurk
A McGurk Mystery

Illustrated by Val Biro

DRAGON
GRANADA PUBLISHING
London Toronto Sydney New York

Published by Granada Publishing Limited
in Dragon Books 1979

ISBN 0 583 30279 3

First published as *Dolls in Danger* by Brockhampton Press
(now Hodder & Stoughton Children's Books) 1974
Text copyright © E. W. Hildick 1974
Illustrations copyright © Hodder & Stoughton 1974

Granada Publishing Limited
Frogmore, St Albans, Herts AL2 2NF
and
3 Upper James Street, London WIR 4BP
1221 Avenue of the Americas, New York, NY 10020, USA
117 York Street, Sydney, NSW 2000, Australia
100 Skyway Avenue, Toronto, Ontario, Canada M9W 3A6
110 Northpark Centre, 2193 Johannesburg, South Africa
CML Centre, Queen & Wyndham, Auckland 1, New Zealand

Made and printed in Great Britain by
Cox & Wyman Ltd,
London, Reading and Fakenham
Set in Intertype Baskerville

For Penelope

Contents

I

Angry voices

Suddenly we heard voices.

Girls' voices – raised up in squeaks and protests.

Angry voices – getting louder and louder and nearer and nearer.

'What is this?' cried McGurk. He stood up and stared at the door that led up into the garden. 'A *lynch* mob?'

The time was 1.59 one summer afternoon.

The place was McGurk's cellar, now headquarters of the McGurk Organization.

The Organization is a detective thing. Maybe you've read about our first case already. McGurk is my best friend and the Organization was his idea. He has lots of good ideas. Also red hair and green eyes. Age ten.

My name is Joey Rockwell. I am in charge of the Organization's records. I can type with four fingers and that's not bad. After all, I have only had the typewriter for three months, one week, and one day. A present for my tenth birthday. I am good at details the way McGurk is good with ideas.

The other members are Willie Sanders and Wanda Grieg.

Willie is not quite ten. Tall and skinny, with a long thin nose. That's what we call him sometimes: The Nose. Willie claims to have a sense of smell that is almost magical, it is so delicate. McGurk believes him. McGurk believes what he wants to believe, and he certainly wants to believe in Willie's wonderful sense of smell. It was this that gave him the idea of a detective organization in the first place. Using Willie as a kind of human bloodhound. A crazy idea, but that's McGurk.

Wanda is nine. Long light-brown hair which *she* calls 'honey-blonde'. She wears old jeans with bright cloth flowers stitched to them. She has a very strange habit for a girl. She likes to climb trees. Especially the big tree in her front garden. She can climb it as good as any boy. Even me.

That takes care of the McGurk Organization personnel, all present that afternoon when the angry voices suddenly started closing in on us. So angry were those voices that even McGurk got alarmed and said, as he tip-toed to the door:

'Hey! I don't like the sound of this.'

But first, just a word about the Organization equipment and then you'll have the complete picture.

Long table; three ordinary chairs; one
    big old rocking chair (McGurk's).
One typewriter (mine); one notebook
    (also mine); one pack of typing paper.
One Movie Make-Up Kit (for if we
    need disguises).
One magnifying glass (which we'd
    bought after solving our first mystery).
And the files: three big cardboard boxes
    labelled (1) MYSTERIES SOLVED; (2)
    LATEST MYSTERY — RECORDS AND
    CLUES; and (3) DETAILS OF SUSPECTS.

Files (2) and (3) were empty. The only mystery we were faced with right then was what all the noise was about in the garden.

'Quiet!' growled McGurk to the rest of us. 'I'm trying to pick out what they're saying.'

2

The ad on the tree

'I was here first!'

'No you were not!'

'She was here first. Then me. You aren't even *second*, Sandra Ennis!'

'Get lost!'

'Just because you're bigger.'

That was what the voices were saying. That was a sample of the sort of things we could hear, coming from the other side of the door. The rest of it you'll just have to imagine. Like the clumps and the scuffs and the scraping and the thudding and the rattle when someone tried the handle.

'What *is* all this?' said McGurk again, looking all around at us and for some reason lighting on me. '*You* know?'

'*I* don't know,' I said. 'Maybe it's just some old game.'

'Not outside our office!' said McGurk, giving a snort. 'Nobody plays games outside a detective organization's office. Not if they know what's good for them.'

He began to turn back to the door.

'Wait!'

Something in Wanda's voice caused McGurk to stop. She was looking hunted.

'You know about this?' asked McGurk.

'Yes.'

'Well?' said McGurk. 'What is it?'

'It's – oh, this'll explain it best,' she said.

Then she took from one of her back pockets a folded piece of paper. And while the clumping and scuffling and arguing went on outside, we gathered round.

'Hey!' I said, before Wanda had got it open, 'that's typing paper. *Our* typing paper.'

'Which my father gave us,' said Willie, glancing at the pile on the table.

'It's a carbon copy!' I said.

'It's an *ad*!' said McGurk, scowling at it, then at Wanda.

'Yes – an advertisement,' said Wanda, not sounding as cool as she seemed to want to sound. 'I wrote it.'

We all read it. (There is a copy over the page.)

'*Your* spelling isn't so bad,' I told Wanda, not noticing the 'reqires' the first time round.

'I borrowed a dictionary,' she said.

'Never mind the education bit!' said McGurk.

'Where d'you place this ad? When? Who gave you permission? You gone daft or something?'

I would have made notes of her answers here, but all these questions in less than two seconds was too much for me. Or Wanda.

She replied by answering a question that nobody had asked yet, but one that some of us were getting round to. Why?

'I thought I'd even things up,' she said.

'Even things *up*?' cried McGurk.

'You heard me. There's no need to yell.'

'*How* even things up, Wanda?' asked Willie.

'I know,' I said. 'It's because she's a girl. Right?'

'Right,' she said. 'Right first time, Joey.'

'This is only my cellar,' said McGurk. 'This is only my organization. *But would somebody mind telling me what it's all about?!*'

'We've come for the interview!' sang out a voice from outside.

'*Not you!*' yelled McGurk. '*Shut up! . . .*' He turned to Wanda. 'Now. So you're a girl. So all right. So what?'

'So I thought being just one girl, and you being three boys, things needed evening up.'

'She means three girls to three boys,' I said.

'Oh, no!' said Wanda. 'Not necessarily. I reckon two girls to three boys will even things up any day.'

'So you do, huh?' growled McGurk, snatching the paper off her and crumpling it up.

'Yes,' said Wanda calmly. 'So I thought if we had a secretary, that would do it. And we do need a secretary. All the organizations need secretaries.'

'We've got Joey here to do that,' said Willie.

'Yes,' I said. 'And nobody – but *no-body* – uses my typewriter. Whatever you decide,' I added, giving McGurk a hard look. It wasn't necessary. That boy had no more notion of going along with Wanda's scheme than I had of jumping on my typewriter.

'So without permission,' he said to Wanda,

14

'you wrote this ad, on the organization's own paper, and you stuck this ad up somewhere for everybody to see?'

'Yes,' said Wanda. 'That's just the copy. The top sheet I nailed to the tree in our front garden. On my way here.'

'Well you can just go—'

'Just a minute, McGurk,' I said. 'There's a question *I'd* like to ask this clever girl, if I may.'

'Go ahead.'

'Why a secretary?' I said to Wanda. 'Why not advertise for another girl detective?'

That got to her. She stiffened up.

'Certainly not!' she said. '*I'm* the girl detective round here.'

'And she calls that *even*,' I said to McGurk and Willie. 'That's girls for you.'

By this time the thumping on the door became very loud and definite.

'Hurry up in there!' came a voice just as hard and definite – the voice of Sandra Ennis. 'It's long past two. Open up!'

Wanda looked pale but defiant. She even had the cheek to grin. She nodded at the door and said:

'Well, fellers, we may not have a *case* on our hands – but we've certainly got a problem!'

3

The siege

'All right!' said McGurk. 'I'll soon clear this mob away. Then we'll deal with *you*!'

And, with a scowl at Wanda, he went and opened the door.

'We're here!'

'Your ad said *prompt*!'

'She wasn't first. I was first.'

'And I was second.'

'Get lost!'

Again, these were the remarks that came from outside. All mixed up and loud and crowded and only possible for a trained expert ear to pick out and remember and write down.

'O.K.! O.K.! Now just listen, girls.'

This was McGurk, arms up and out and braced against the doorposts.

They quietened down a bit. The rest of us looked out between McGurk's arms.

Well, there was a queue of girls. If you can call it a queue with all that shoving going on. It looked as if there were a hundred out there on those four steps leading down from the garden. But really there were only seven. I started making a list of their names:

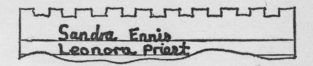

McGurk went on talking:
'There's been a mistake.'
They all started groaning. Sandra said:
'You mean we should come at two *tomorrow*?'
And the groaning stopped and I wrote down four more names.

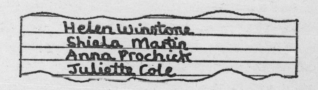

'No, it's just a big mistake,' McGurk said. 'There's been a mistake.'
And that did it.
Somebody at the back said, 'Great joke!' and shoved those in front of her. It was Manya Handley. And since she was shoving downhill it had quite a big effect, sending Sandra Ennis

bang into McGurk's arms, McGurk back into my notebook, and the end of her own name right out of my list:

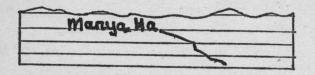

'Hey now, take it easy!' cried McGurk. 'Somebody might get hurt.'

'Kids!' said Sandra Ennis, still clinging to McGurk and smiling patiently. 'Fine secretaries *they'd* make.'

Well I saw through her right away. Because as anybody who knows Sandra Ennis could tell you, this was her big Charm Act. She puts it on all the time when she wants her own way, and honestly, sometimes at school it gets *nauseating*. I mean really *obnoxious*. And what makes it specially nauseating and obnoxious is that she gets away with it so often. With grown-ups. It's that fair curly hair, lighter than corn, and those big blue eyes, and those dark fluttery lashes, and two of the biggest rottenest dimples you ever saw.

'Never mind that riff-raff, McGurk,' she said. 'I'm the one for the job. I can do shorthand.'

'What?' cried Wanda.

'My own special brand,' said Sandra, ignoring her and fluttering at McGurk. 'And because I knew you'd not be looking any further,' she said, 'I pulled the notice down and here it is.'

McGurk ignored it.

'We don't want a secretary,' he said.

Sandra's fluttering slowed down a bit, and her voice hardened a little.

'This says you do,' she said, rustling the paper under his nose.

'Maybe,' said McGurk. 'But *I* didn't put that thing up.'

'Well one of your organization did. I saw her doing it.'

'Maybe. But it was against my orders and without my – my—'

'Knowledge?' I suggested.

'Yer,' said McGurk. 'Without my knowledge even.'

Now the fluttering of Sandra's lashes increased again. Her eyes flashed through them and over McGurk's shoulder at Wanda.

'Well sack her then. And I'll take her place.'

'Now you just watch it, or—'

'Back! back!' said McGurk, turning and pushing Wanda away. 'It would serve you right if I *did*. . . . But no,' he said to Sandra. 'I'm sorry. No vacancies. Either for secretaries or girl officers. Sorry, girls,' he said to those hanging back behind Sandra. 'Same goes for you all. It's just been a mistake.'

There were one or two grunts, but for a second it looked as if they might go quietly.

Then Sandra turned nasty. To the girls she'd been bossing and shoving around earlier, she suddenly became friendly.

'Now you stay around, girls,' she said. 'They advertised for interviews and interviews is what they're going to give us. All of us.'

'That's what you think,' said McGurk, stepping back and grabbing the door.

But he wasn't quick enough.

Sandra stepped forward and wedged herself there, shouting:

'Come on, girls! Gimme a hand!'

Some of them did at that. I mean they may not have thought much of Sandra Ennis, but they'd been fooled as much as she had.

'This—' panted McGurk, when he found the wedge too tight, 'this is a breach of the peace. Trespassing. Breaking and entering.'

'So what?' jeered Sandra. 'This is *fraud*!'

She waved the notice in his face with such a swipe that he ducked, and Sandra's hand and the notice went over his head and clipped Willie on the nose.

'Hey! That – that was my *dose*!' he cried, clapping a hand to it.

'You ought to get it cut short then,' was all she replied.

'Ha!' yelled McGurk. 'That was a deliberate assault!'

'Yes,' I said. 'On an officer of the law. Is it bleeding, Willie?'

'Duh-doe. Bud id *nearly* is!' said Willie.

'Officer of the law!' jeered Sandra.

'He is *too*!' said McGurk. 'We all are, in this organization. Look!'

And he pulled out his I.D. card and flashed it at her.

Well, of course, he was getting carried away. Short of cases the way we were, McGurk was glad of any kind of crime to deal with. He was also glad of the opportunity to flash that card.

And no wonder. I'd spent a lot of time typing our I.D. cards. What with our ages and heights and other details and a snapshot of the officer and his fingerprints, they looked very classy.

Sandra Ennis, though, was in no mood to appreciate art.

She took one look at McGurk's card, and said: 'Yergh!' – snatched it off him, sandwiched it with the notice, and tore them both in half.

Then she lifted her hands and let the four pieces fall on McGurk's head.

And that was *her* big mistake.

No. McGurk didn't hit her. McGurk has never once hit a girl on purpose, I'll say that for him. But what he *did* – well, some people might say it was worse.

'Right!' he said, slow and gritty and not very loud. 'Right! Just hold 'em, men. I'll be right back.'

The girls didn't give us much trouble. They pushed just hard enough to stop us from closing the door and – led by Sandra – started a chant:

'He's gone to fetch his Mammy! He's gone to fetch his Mammy!'

Well I knew McGurk wouldn't do that either. But the girls were shoving hard enough for the three of us – Willie, Wanda, and myself – to be kept busy shoving back. So we didn't have a chance to turn our heads and see what McGurk *had* gone to fetch.

'RIGHT! GET OUT!' we heard him roar, behind us.

Sandra's mouth dropped open in mid-chant. Helen Winstone went white. Leonora Priest screamed.

'OUT! OUT! OUT!' came McGurk's roar, nearer.

By now the pressure was definitely off.

We were able to turn round.

'Oh!' gasped Wanda, going pale herself.

'Whu-what—?' stammered Willie.

Even I was shattered.

Because something that looked like a Fish Monster was approaching. Like McGurk it had red hair and freckles and green eyes. But the rest of it? A great slimy mouth covered the whole bottom half of his face and went stretching behind his neck. A creature from another planet. Aquarius. Horrible.

Espccially when it spoke and a huge lolling tongue rolled out, and great slabs of teeth jutted up and down.

'GET OUT! OUT! OUT!'

They knew it was McGurk all right. They soon realized it was a magnifying glass in front of his mouth. But it still looked horrible.

Then one of them shouted:

'He's going to chase us!'

'I'M GOING TO EAT YA!' roared the mouth.

And they all ran off, squealing, some of them *hoping* he would chase them.

But McGurk closed the door.

'Wow!' he said.

'For heaven's *sake*!' cried Wanda, for he'd still got the glass in front of his mouth.

'wow! wow!' he said, keeping it there just to punish her.

Then he put the glass on the table and we got down to business.

4

A client

'All right,' Wanda kept saying, 'all right. So I shouldn't have done it. But it created some *interest*, didn't it?'

'That kind of interest we can do without,' McGurk kept saying to that.

But because Wanda didn't give McGurk a real argument, he didn't get mad. Instead he explained. I think it made him feel good to explain. I think he'd decided that any boss could get mad, but only the real high-class ones go on and on and on explaining.

'You see, it's not *girls* I object to becoming new members. It's *anybody*.'

'All right,' Wanda kept saying. 'I heard you *first* time.'

'Yer, well, it's true,' said McGurk. 'It makes sense.'

'Yes. Sure. I agree. I—'

'It makes sense because we have to keep the numbers down. A detective organization should never—'

'Get too big. Right. I heard you first time. I *agree*, McGurk. I agree.'

It was Wanda who was sounding mad now.

But McGurk went on.

'A detective organization should never get too big. Four is enough. How can we work in secret if every kid in the neighbourhood is a member?'

'Right. We can't. McGurk, you made your point. All right?'

'And four is enough,' said McGurk again. 'Sometimes I think it's too many.'

'And you stretched a point,' said Wanda, looking very tight in the lips. 'Don't forget that bit, McGurk. You only said it *five* times already.'

'Huh?'

'How you all stretched a point letting me – a mere girl – become a member.'

'Oh. That. Yer. Well I said that before. And so we *did* stretch a point. Didn't we, Jocy? Didn't we, Willie?'

We nodded.

Wanda blew a kind of snort through her nose.

'Well—' she began, and I think she was so mad she was just about to throw in her I.D. card and go climb her tree.

Then McGurk said:

'Mind you, it was a very good decision. Right, fellers?'

Sure, we nodded. Sure.

'I mean we'd rather have you in the organization than any of the boys who've been wanting to join.'

'Oh?' said Wanda, looking interested instead of mad. 'Boys have been wanting to join?'

'Pleading,' said McGurk.

'Begging,' I said.

'Yer,' said Willie.

'Like who?'

'Like Bert Rafferty, Tom Camuty, Jerry Pierce . . .'

'Oh,' said Wanda. She looked *much* happier now. 'But you wouldn't have them?'

'No way,' said McGurk.

'Some of them got mad,' said Willie.

'Creeps,' said McGurk.

'So you see, Wanda,' I said, 'it's a real privilege for *any* of us.'

'Yer,' said Willie.

'And it's my cellar,' said McGurk.

So that about wrapped it up, and we went quiet for a while (apart from my typewriter making out a new I.D. card for McGurk), and we all felt good.

It was about thirty minutes later that the quiet time ended.

A knock came at the door.

Light, not loud, but very fast.

'See who that is, Willie,' said McGurk.

Willie opened the door. Just a crack at first, and shielding his nose. I suppose he still wasn't sure Sandra Ennis wouldn't be back for another swipe.

'Come on, come on!' said a girl's voice. 'Open up, why don't you?'

It was a thin squeaky voice, but very fierce.

'It's little Ally Merrick,' said Wanda, without turning round.

Willie opened the door wider. He must have

felt safe. If little Ally, who is only six and small for her age – if she'd stood on tip-toe and swung a cricket bat at it, she could hardly have reached that nose.

'Come on! Take me to McGurk!'

'Go away, Ally,' said McGurk, without stopping his rocking. 'It's all a mistake. We don't need a secretary.'

'Seggerderry?' Ally poked her head round the door, all pale under the tight black curls. 'Hallo, Wanda . . . What's a segger – seggra – what you just said, McGurk? You're detectives, aren't you?'

'Yes.' McGurk had stopped rocking. He was leaning forward, looking interested. 'Sure we're detectives, Ally. Why?'

'That's all right then,' said Ally, pushing past Willie and coming to the table. 'Because I have a mystery for you.'

'Yes? Go on.'

'What is it, Ally?' asked Wanda, gently.

Suddenly Ally's eyes crinkled up.

'My – my youngest daughter!' she sobbed. 'She – she's been kidnapped!'

5

The missing dolls

'Yergh!' groaned Willie. 'She means a doll!'

'Ku-ku-kidnapped!' sobbed Ally, nodding her head so hard the tears flew all over my typing.

McGurk sank back.

'And I thought we had a case,' he said.

'Maybe it's a plot,' I said. 'Maybe the older girls sent her.'

'Be quiet!' snapped Wanda. 'All of you! Can't you see she's genuinely upset?' She crouched down in front of Ally. 'Tell *me* about it, pet,' she said. 'Who says it's been kidnapped? Which doll? When did it happen?'

After a bit more sobbing and a lot more tears, Ally managed to answer some of the questions. I was already taking notes.

'It *wasn't* a doll,' Ally said at first. 'It was Maria. My youngest daughter.'

Then more sobbing.

'O.K., O.K. Now which one is Maria? I forget.'

'She's – she's my baby. She drinks and – and she wets – and – and she sings.'

'Sings?' said McGurk.

'She did,' said Ally, 'befuh – befuh – before her illness. She used to sing White Christmas. And she can look sideways. That's why I put her there.'

'Put her where, pet?'

'Bottom of – front drive. On the grass. To – to watch out for the postman.'

'The postman?'

'Yuh-yes. She – she liked that. She – she was expecting a letter.'

'A *baby*? Expecting a *letter*?'

McGurk was looking impatient. He rolled his eyes and twinkled a get-rid-of-her sign with his fingers.

'Yes,' said Ally, still snuffling on Wanda's shoulder. 'About a new part. For the singing. Under grinty.'

'What's that?' I said.

I was finding it hard, trying to make notes fast enough.

Wanda turned and whispered the answer.

'Under *guarantee*. The doll. Dee-oh-ell-ell . . . She's right. I heard her mother say they'd written to the manufacturer.'

'So anyway,' said McGurk, 'she's missing.'

'Kidnapped!' said Ally, looking up and glaring at him.

'When?' said McGurk.

'Minute ago,' said Ally.

'Now hold it,' I said. 'You've been *here* more than a minute.'

'Put "In the last hour or so," ' said Wanda.

'Yes,' said Ally. 'Put that.'

'When did you last *see* the d– the child?' said McGurk.

'Before Mummy rang the bell.'

'The lunch bell, pet?'

'Yes. The lunch bell.'

'You sure?'

'Yes. Because Maria was hungry. But I said no. You – you wait there. Watch out for the postman. And – and – it's all – muh-my fuh-*fault*!'

'O.K., O.K. ... Take it easy. It's not your fault at *all*, pet. Did you go straight out after lunch?'

'Minute ago,' sobbed Ally.

'And Maria wasn't there, hmm?'

'No. Gone. Kidnapped.'

'Right!' said McGurk, standing up. 'We'll take the case. Kidnapped – swiped – just lost – we'll find your – er – baby. You got the details, Joey?'

I nodded.

'So let's go inspect the scene of the crime,' said McGurk. 'While it's still fresh.'

'It could be that dog again,' said Willie, meaning the Henshaws' beagle.

'No!' said Wanda. 'They're on holiday.'

'Cut the yacking,' said McGurk. 'Let's investigate.'

We all began to move towards the door. But before we could get there – some more knocking.

This time McGurk opened it.

'Yes?'

It was another little girl. Marni Williams. Also six. Fair hair in plaits. Blue eyes in tears.

'Don't tell me *you've* had a doll snatched?'

'Nu-no!' snivelled Marni, hanging her head. 'It's my little girl . . .'

'Your little girl then,' said McGurk. 'She been kidnapped?'

'No. She – she—'

'Tell me about it, pet,' said Wanda, going into her crouch again and offering the girl her dry shoulder.

This time it was a rag doll. This time the 'mother' really felt guilty.

'I'd been – I'd been hitting her again.'

'Hitting her?'

'Yes – oh, yes, Wanda! It's my fault. I shouldn't have! I shouldn't have! I hit her and kicked her and pulled her hair and thumped her and then I threw her over the bush in the front garden. And – and then – after lunch when I went to love her and kiss her and tell her how good she was – shu-she – shu-she . . .'

(Break for tears, with the other little kid joining in.)

Then Marni managed to spit it out.

'She wasn't there no more. And nobody knew where she'd gone. But I know. Oh, I've been so cruel! Oh, I shouldn't have treated her like that! Because now – now she's run away from *home*!'

'That may be,' growled McGurk. 'But two on the same day – and both since lunch – looks like we're *really* in business, fellers. Come on.'

35

6

Clues and descriptions

What McGurk was in such a hurry for us to do, of course, was look for clues.

What else?

That is what detectives always do.

But me, I have my own ideas about clues.

Like this time for instance.

Off we went, tramping all round the spots where those little kids had last seen their dolls. Off we went, crawling round those front gardens on our hands and knees, in the area McGurk marked out for us. Off we went on our careful search, getting in one another's way, and having to stop every two minutes to shoo away the little kids and their little kid friends and dogs and I don't know what all. Off we went, doing all this, with all these spectators, including some bigger kids, like Jerry Pierce and Shiela Martin. Jeering at us and asking us things like were we *grazing* down there on the grass.

And, after all this, did we find any clues?

Course we found clues!

We found so many clues we filled two of those big envelopes with them.

I tell you: you can *always* find clues. Anywhere. Anytime. Go out now and try if you don't believe me.

But the trouble is: WHAT DO YOU DO WITH THEM WHEN YOU HAVE THEM?

I said that to McGurk, when we got back.

'O.K., McGurk,' I said. 'Now we've collected all these clues, what next?'

'We examine them,' he said. 'Figure them out. Build up a picture.'

'Right,' I said. 'Here goes.'

And I tipped out on to the table all the clues we'd gathered in the Merricks' garden, on the grass near the end of the drive.

'I see it all,' I said, shuffling the clues around. 'The snatcher came along eating ice lollies. Three,' I said, tapping the sticks. 'Two strawberry and one orange.' I pointed to the coloured stains. 'A real three-ice-lolly man. An ice-lolly-sandwich sucker. So all right. So he's just coming to the end and he sees Ally's doll. "Aha!" he says. "I'll snatch this and maybe the ransom money will keep me in ice lollies the rest of my life!" So he tosses down the ice-lolly sticks and looks all round—'

'Now listen,' McGurk began – but I was swinging now. I was really beginning to *see* this picture.

'And now,' I said, 'now he's at the nervous bit, the dangerous bit. So he has a smoke to steady his nerves. He takes out his last cigarette—' I held up the butt – 'which is a Woodbine. He takes it out of this packet—' I held up the crumpled object that McGurk himself had been so excited to find – 'which happens to be an Embassy packet. But don't let that fool you, men. That helps narrow it down. It's not everyone keeps his Woodbines in an Embassy packet. All we have to do—'

'Very funny!' said McGurk, not meaning it one little bit.

Well I'd made my point. And I had to admit that it made me feel better to be able to put something into File Number Two at last: the one that said LATEST MYSTERY – RECORDS AND CLUES.

And anyway, the CLUES bit wasn't really my side of the operation and the RECORDS were. So I got busy recording the details of the two crimes:

Report Number One

```
MISSING OBJECT/PERSON:  Baby doll
NAME (if any):          Maria
OWNER/NEXT OF KIN:      Alison Merrick
ADDRESS:                31 Elm Close
LAST SEEN (LOCATION):   Front garden, end
     of drive, above address ,
LAST SEEN (TIME):    Approx. 12.30 p.m.
             Tuesday, August 8
DESCRIPTION (GENERAL): Baby. Blue eyes.
             Pink dress. No shoes.
DESCRIPTION (SPECIAL POINTS): Wets when
     fed and tilted forward.  Speech de-
     fect. (Used to sing White Christmas
     when control at back turned.  Now
     only makes a whirring noise.)
```

Report Number Two

```
MISSING OBJECT/PERSON:  Girl Doll
NAME (if any):          Ann (Raggedy)
OWNER/NEXT OF KIN:      Marni Williams
ADDRESS:                21 Elm Close
LAST SEEN (LOCATION):   Front garden,
     flying over bush towards street,
             above address
LAST SEEN(TIME):   Approx. 1.00 p.m.
             Tuesday, August 8
DESCRIPTION (GENERAL): Rag doll.  Red
     and white checked dress. White
     calico long drawers (with lace.)
     Yellow hair (silk cord)
DESCRIPTION (SPECIAL POINTS): Left eye
     (black button) missing
```

And if you think typing all that out was a good afternoon's work, forget it. Because while I was finishing the second of those cards, news of two more snatches came in.

Report Number Three

```
MISSING OBJECT/PERSON:   Toy Bear
NAME (if any):   Eduardo (alias Teddy)
OWNER/NEXT OF KIN:        Sue Gallon
ADDRESS:              40 Olive Drive
LAST SEEN (LOCATION):  On clothes line at
    back of gallons' garage. (Hanging to dry
    after being taken for swim in tub
    because of the heat.)
LAST SEEN (TIME):   4.20 p.m. Tuesday,
                    August 8
DESCRIPTION (GENERAL):  Teddy bear, ordinary
        size.  No clothes but thick yellow
        fur.  Rather sharp nose
DESCRIPTION (SPECIAL POINTS): Still wet.
        Operation scar. (30 black stitches
        across abdomen, when operated on for a
        bust squeaker, the time when McGurk
        made his cellar into a hospital
        operating theatre.)
        Squeaker still doesn't work
```

Report Number Four

```
MISSING OBJECT/PERSON:   Teeny Doll
NAME (if any):           Marcella
OWNER/NEXT OF KIN:       Manya Handley
ADDRESS:             15 Braddock Grove
LAST SEEN (LOCATION): In basket in front
    of handlebars of Manya's bicycle,
    when left for few minutes outside
    Turner's sweet shop
LAST SEEN (TIME): 5.05 p.m. Tuesday,
                  August 8
DESCRIPTION (GENERAL):  Teenage, but small
    (12" tall).  Silver-blonde nylon hair,
    windswept style.  Yellow cotton dress
    with purple belt.  Orange knee boots
    (real suede)
DESCRIPTION (SPECIAL POINTS):  Blue eyes
    (open and shut type) with long black
    lashes and slightly crossed
SPECIAL REMARKS (by Officer Grieg):  "At
    age 11 you might think Manya too old
    for making such a fuss over a doll.
    But she says it is her lucky mascot
    and its loss will ruin her chances
    for the rest of her life."
```

Four snatches. All in one day.

7

A bag job?

'Well,' said McGurk, at six that evening, after we had gathered four more envelopes of clues. (Three of them from outside Turners' sweet shop, which just has to be the best place for clues in the whole of this town.)

'Well,' he said (and it took him all this time to say it because he was thinking very hard), 'it's got me beat. Only for the moment, mind you,' he said quickly. 'But yes – I don't mind admitting it, men. For the moment it's got me beat.'

'Me too,' said Willie, sighing.

'You can say that again,' said Wanda, sadly.

I was too busy looking over my record cards to say anything yet. I had my ideas, though.

'I mean,' said McGurk, 'who *could* have done it? Nobody's seen any strangers lurking round.'

'So it must be someone from the neighbourhood,' Wanda said.

'Yes,' said McGurk. 'I was coming to that ... But *who*?'

'That's the mystery,' said Willie.

'And that's what we've been wanting,' said Wanda. 'A mystery.'

'Then Item Number Two,' said McGurk, holding up another finger. 'Nobody's seen anyone picking up any of those dolls. Or carrying them around. In broad daylight.'

'Sounds like an invisible man,' said Willie. 'Like on telly last week, when—'

'Willie,' said McGurk, 'do you *mind*?'

'Sorry,' said Willie.

'This is no joke,' said Wanda, feeling her damp shoulders.

'I wasn't joking,' said Willie.

'Willie!' said McGurk. 'That's even worse!'

And now I decided it was time for me to throw some light on the subject.

'Could have been a bag job,' I said.

'Huh?' said McGurk.

'A bag job. In fact I might put that in my report. *Probable M.O.: bag snatch.*'

'What's this M.O.?' said Willie.

'The way it was done,' I said. 'It's what the police put for the way a crime has been done.'

'Method of operation,' said Wanda.

'Something like that,' I said. 'Anyway, a bag

42

job. Just an ordinary brown paper bag. Folded up. Out of sight. Concealed on person. Then a likely victim shows up. Nobody looking. Out

with bag, open up, in with victim – done. The criminal goes on his way carrying what looks like an ordinary bag of groceries . . . apples . . . eggs . . . pint of milk . . . anything.'

'Yer!' said Willie. 'Or a bottle of gin, or—'

'Or maybe *nobody's* snatched the dolls,' said McGurk, leering round. 'How about *that*?'

I *thought* he'd been taking my theory (which

43

you have to admit was a brilliant one) very calmly, not at all jealous. And now I knew the reason: *that bloke had one of his own ready all the time.*

'Yer,' said Willie, 'like I said – an invisible being—'

'No, Willie,' I said. 'That's not what McGurk means. I know what he means,' I said, trying not to look as if I wished I'd thought of it first. 'It's a thought, McGurk,' I said, being very fair. 'You mean—'

'I mean these four kids might only be *pretending*,' said McGurk. 'Just to make a game of it.'

'Well I think that's stupid!' said Wanda. 'Those tears were real enough.' She shrugged her shoulders and plucked the cloth of her shirt away from them, shivering a little. Then she said: 'Look, I don't know about you fellers, but I'm going home to change and see what's for supper.'

And that's when we called it a day, even though we were still not sure of the nature of the crime when we split. We still couldn't say whether it was a straight *stealing* job, or a *spite* affair (we hadn't yet checked the victims for enemies), or (and never mind what Wanda said, in my book little girls can make real tears any time) a false crime wave.

But we hadn't long to find out.

No, sir.

The next time we all met in that office, the following morning, we knew for sure.

And we had real evidence to prove it.

In writing.

8

The note

I was late getting to the office the next morning. It was 10.30 by the time I arrived. I'd been to the dentist.

And when I went through that door into the McGurks' cellar, I could see at a glance that something had happened. Something big.

The others were all three bending over the table. McGurk was in the middle and he was holding the magnifying glass and studying an envelope there.

'Come on, McGurk!' Wanda was saying. 'Let somebody else have a turn.'

'Yes!' said Willie.

'Be quiet!' said McGurk. 'This is important ... Hallo!' he said, looking up at me. 'Come see what's arrived while you've been absent.'

'A note,' said Willie.

'A ransom note,' said Wanda.

I could see that. It was plainly printed on that envelope – a big brown envelope similar to those we used for clues. Except this one had a label and the label said:

Like that.

The printing cut out of newspapers and magazines.

'So,' I said, 'where's the note itself? How did it arrive? When?'

I was already clicking my pen ready and reaching for the notebook.

'Someone tossed it into the basket on Manya Handley's bike,' said McGurk. 'While she was over at the Gallons'.'

'When she came out to the bike it was lying there in the basket,' said Wanda.

'Nobody saw anybody,' said Willie.

'And the note itself, the note?'

'Here,' said McGurk, drawing it carefully out of the envelope with the tips of his fingers.

'I don't know what you're fussing like that for,' said Wanda. 'Anyone careful enough to disguise their writing this way won't have left any prints.'

'And even if they have,' I said, 'we haven't got any way of dealing with them. So open up, McGurk, *please*.'

Still being very careful, not taking any notice of what we'd said, he opened it out.

The McGurk ORganisation is NO GOOD. If mcguRk and Other 3 do not admit this in writeING AND tAck admission to GRieg's Tree by noon Friday Dolls are doomed. misTER Big

'So there it is, Joey,' said McGurk. 'Now we have a motive.'

'To make *us* look small,' said Wanda.

'By Mister Big,' said Willie.

'And now we know what we're up against,' said McGurk, his eyes all aglow. 'A real high-powered Criminal Master Mind.' He rubbed his hands. 'I like that, I like that! But—' he slapped the note that he'd been so careful with up until then – 'we'll *see* who has the Master Mind round here.'

'You tell 'em, McGurk!' said Willie.

McGurk seemed so pleased, I had to give him a hard look to make sure it wasn't something he'd dreamed up himself. Wanda was also looking sideways at him. We knew him better than Willie did.

But no. He seemed too genuinely pleased with the challenge.

So I flipped open my notebook.

'Did Manya bring it personally?'

'Course. Who else?'

'Had she read it!' I asked.

'Well of course!' said McGurk. 'What do *you* think? Course she'd read it.'

'Ha-hmm!' I said, noting this down and frowning. 'So how did she feel about it?'

'What difference does *that* make?' said

McGurk. '*I* don't know. She seemed, well—'

'Pleased, really,' said Wanda. 'Still upset but pleased to know the doll was still unharmed. Why? Do you still think it's a false alarm? That she did it and wrote this herself? Because you're wrong. She really and truly—'

'No, no,' I said. 'I'm thinking something much worse than that ... Listen. Do the other kids know about it?'

'Yes!' said McGurk. 'The Gallon kids knew as soon as she did and by now they'll have blabbed it all around.' He was looking annoyed. 'So cut the fooling, Joey, and stop looking mysterious ... Men,' he said, turning to the others, 'we have something to work on now. And – like I was saying before Joey came – my feeling is that this Mister Big is one of the blokes who're always ribbing us about the organization.'

'Right!' said Willie. 'Those who're mad be-cause—'

'Like those three creeps we were talking about yesterday, for instance,' said McGurk, with a grim nod. 'Get this down, Joey. Prime Suspects – Bert Rafferty, Jerry Pierce, and Tom Camuty. Whass matter? Am I going too fast for you?'

'No. But don't you see—'

'Well get their names down then. Then we'll draw up a schedule for checking on them, their

movements. We'll pull them in for questioning—'

'Yes, and all their friends,' said Wanda, hooked on McGurk's enthusiasm.

'And – and we'll work out a detail for *shadowing* them, eh, McGurk?' said Willie. 'Like you were saying—'

'But listen, *will* you?' I cried. 'Don't you see what all this *means*? Don't you see the *trouble* we're in?'

'Trouble?!' said McGurk glaring at me. 'What trouble? We now have a wonderful lead here—' he slapped the note '—and *he* talks about trouble. What trouble? Come on, come on, spit it out, feller! *What* trouble?'

'Well,' I began . . .

But I didn't need to go any further.

Because just then the trouble I was going to tell them about came FLOOM! – right down upon us where we stood.

9

The trouble

It came in the shape of Mrs McGurk.

Polite knock. Nice lady. Dark and quiet and thin, not like McGurk. But brisk and with a tight look about her smile, as if it could be switched off – click! – like that.

'Hello, Mum,' said McGurk. 'We're a bit busy just now, but—'

'I'm sure you are,' she said. 'That's a nice shirt, Wanda. Hello, Willie, Joey . . .'

This was sounding very ominous to me.

'I've just had a call from Mrs Handley—'

'Oh, yes?' McGurk flicked his fingers for me to get busy and take notes. 'What does she say?'

'She says that *she's* just had a call from Mrs Gallon—'

'Ha!' said McGurk. 'About these dolls?'

The fool! He was even looking glad.

'Yes,' said Mrs McGurk, 'about the dolls. And they both say, and I agree, and I'm sure the other two mothers will also agree, that—'

'Aw, gosh, Mum,' smirked McGurk, 'they

don't have to thank us! It's a pleasure to take up the case. It's our *duty* to take up the case.'

'That isn't what they were saying. They were saying, and I agree, that it's gone on long enough. A game's a game, but to those little girls it isn't.'

Now it was getting through to him. Suddenly his forehead wrinkled up into his arguing expression.

'Yes, but Mum,' he said, '*we* haven't got the dolls. *We* didn't snatch them. Hah, fellers?'

We shook our heads but it was a losing battle. Mrs McGurk smiled tightly on and said:

'No. I know that. But I hear that all you have to do is—' she bent her head to the note, then straightened up – 'yes, this is what I was told. All you have to do is what it says there and the girls get their dolls back.'

'That's ALL?!'

'Now you know what your father says about shouting like that!'

'Yes, but Mum – you mean you want us to – to give *in*? To do *this*?'

The smile came back.

'Yes. Why not? It may be only a game to you, but to those little girls it's not. It's very important. It's—'

'But to *us* it's important too. Very, very important. Right, men?'

'Yes,' I said, 'but this is what I was meaning.'

'We *would* look fools,' said Wanda, doubtfully.

'Grade One fools,' said Willie.

Mrs McGurk addressed us all.

'So you'd be prepared to let harm come to those dolls just for the sake of—?'

'Nergh!' cried McGurk. 'I mean certainly not, Mum. Who said anything about *that*? Look. Stop worrying, Mum. We have until Friday noon, right? O.K. Well if we can't bust this case by then – now that we have all *this* to go on – why,' he said, 'well then we *deserve* to write that admission. Men?'

'Right!'

'Yes, he's right, Mrs McGurk.'

'Yes, *ma'am*!'

The smile wobbled a bit. Maybe she hadn't expected it to be four against one.

'Well,' she said slowly, 'well – all right then. So long as you *remember* that.'

Then she left us. Nice lady. A bit meddling, like all grown-ups. But not too pushy.

So anyway, there we were. That was the trouble I'd been trying to warn the others about and now they all knew it.

If we didn't solve this case, if we didn't track down this 'Mister Big' and get those dolls back before Friday noon, we would just have to do what the note said.

And that was a HORRIBLE thought.

Really OBNOXIOUS.

But it still seemed a long way to Friday. And McGurk – trust *him*! – he soon brightened up.

'Right!' he said. 'About those three prime suspects. Here's what we do . . .'

Ques

Pull
Ha

Shadow

First, noboay
ing. Pulling prime
may be all right for regula
have the Law to fall back on, a.
force if necessary. But not the McG
ization. No, sir.

So what questioning was done, was done ou
there in the streets. Walking alongside the prime
suspect. Being polite to him if necessary. Even
offering him a sweet to get him willing to talk.
Even listening to his lip.

For the record, I did make a few notes. Here is
a specimen of one of those sessions, how it started:

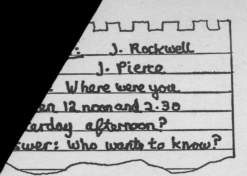

: J. Rockwell

J. Pierce

: Where were you
en 12 noon and 2.30
erday afternoon?
swer: Who wants to know?

away, you see, the suspect starts asking
ons *himself*.

ell, after that point my writing gets wilder,

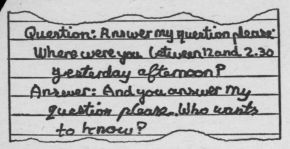

Question: Answer my question please.
Where were you between 12 and 2.30
yesterday afternoon?
Answer: And you answer my
question please. Who wants
to know?

but this is how the session ended up:

Q. So how about it, Jerry? Where were you
yesterday at the times stated?
A. Well, having lunch, I suppose.
Q. *All* the time, Jerry?
A. No. Before lunch and after lunch I was with
Bert Rafferty.
Q. Aha! What *doing*?

58

A. Hey, now! Wait a bit! Why pick on *me*? Why don't you ask Bert himself?

So little Jerry Pierce got the last question after all. The creep.

The session with Bert Rafferty, McGurk handled himself. I was with him but I only took notes. And here it is. The whole bit. All on one page.

INTERROGATOR: J. McGurk
SUSPECT: B. Rafferty
Q. What were you doing yesterday between 12 and 2.30?
A. Flying a kite.
Q. Oh? Who with?
A. Donald Duck.
Q. Don't get clever.
R.A. Who's getting clever?

There! See it? The suspect starts asking the questions again. So I had to start putting R. for Rafferty and M. for McGurk instead of Q. and A.

M. You're getting clever.
R I am, am I?
M. Yes. You are. So—
R. So get lost, McGurk.

59

Then Rafferty turned up into his own garden and that was the end of that session.

Tom Camuty we couldn't even get to *begin* to answer our questions.

Shadowing them was an even bigger mess.

Shadowing is also all right for regular police. It is even all right for citizens, but only in busy cities. In busy cities you have street corners and doorways and parked cars and crowds of people to dodge in and out of and behind and around. Shadowing must be a cinch there. But not in a neighbourhood like ours: wide empty streets, not many people around, everything fairly quiet.

Bushes, yes. We used bushes until we got sick of bushes. But even these were no good, what with kids like Sue Gallon shouting, 'Hello there, Joey! What you doing behind that bush?' – and old grouches like Grandad Martin banging on the window and hollering, 'Hey! You there, boy! You stealing my gooseberries again? Now you clear off, you hear?'

And then there was the question of numbers.

There are four of us, right?

And there were only three prime suspects, right?

So there was no sweat about numbers, right?

WRONG!

Because those three blokes had friends. And since they all knew we were shadowing them, what was to stop them sending their *friends* off to snatch a doll or two? And the total of prime suspects and friends (and I'm talking about their *best* friends now) came to twelve.

Get it?

Twelve of *them*, and only four of *us*.

As Wanda said at the end of the afternoon, when we all met up in the office, bushed – bushed from all that bushwork:

'Maybe *now* you wish there were more than four of us in the organization, McGurk?'

He didn't bother to reply.

He'd been insulted by Bert Rafferty. He'd been deliberately led a long long dance by Jerry Pierce, all round the park. And he'd had a fight with two of Tommy Camuty's pals, having been led into an ambush by Tommy. He *said* he'd won, of course, but he looked pretty roughed up to me.

Anyway, what I'm getting at is this.

Was McGurk downhearted?

Was he ready for giving in?

No, sir.

'It's only Wednesday evening,' he said. 'We still have all the time in the world.'

'Yes, like a day and a half,' I said.

He ignored that remark.

'And tomorrow we'll try a completely different approach,' he said. 'Don't worry, men.'

Black Thursday – Part One

Thursday was the next day and Thursday was a *terrible* day. Right up until the middle of the afternoon it was, anyway. And because the time was running out, I did my record for that day in log-book form. Just to be able to see at a glance how near to disaster we were getting. Like this:

8.30 a.m. Met in McGurk's cellar. Everyone looked nervous except McGurk. McGurk tells us of latest Great Idea.

'We must take a census, men. A census of all the neighbourhood dolls.'

'What's a census?' asks Willie.

'A count, he means,' says Wanda.

'Not just a count,' I say, 'but also a list of those dolls. Right, McGurk?'

McGurk says yes. Just a brief description and name and address of owner. I nod. I see. It is not all *that* great, but it makes sense.

'My feeling is that Mister Big will strike again,' he says. 'Between now and the deadline he will snatch some more. And if we have a list of dolls we might be able to second-guess which ones he'll try for next.'

'How?' says Willie.

'By looking to see if there's a pattern,' says McGurk. He points to the street map. 'Like if he's making sketches in some sort of pattern, street by street.'

'Yes,' I say, beginning to get excited, 'or if he's aiming at certain types of dolls.'

'Or at certain owners,' says Wanda.

'That's what I mean,' says McGurk. 'And if we have a full list, we can make our guesses more accurate.'

'And then catch him—'

'Red-handed,' says McGurk. 'So go to it, men. Joey: you take Olive Drive. Wanda: Elm Close. Willie . . .'

Willie is the only one who isn't enthusiastic. Maybe he's too dim to understand about patterns and check-lists and predictions. All he can say is this:

'Well. Seems to me Mister Big just snatches a doll when he sees his chance. Without any old pattern or list or street map. But you're the boss.'

10.30 a.m. Just about now I am beginning to wonder if Willie hasn't more sense than the rest

64

put together. Census? Brief descriptions? Listen, this is going to take us *years*. And why?

1. Because some of these girls have more than twenty dolls each. No kidding. Sue Gallon has twenty-four! (Twenty-five with the missing bear.) And 2. because they all have names and special descriptions. Even the baby dolls, which all look alike to me.

So at this time I have only done one half of one side of the street.

12.00 noon. We meet again. The others have been finding the same snags. So, like me, they started speeding up: cutting down on descriptions, leaving out dolls that aren't really dolls but old strips of blanket and home-made stuff like that.

Result: four lists that look like kites – full at the top and then long and stringy after that.

'Don't worry, men,' says McGurk. 'Another hour after lunch should see us through. There's only Braddock Grove left.'

12.05 p.m. Knock at the door. Two little girls. Evie Taylor and Alice Sherwood. Two more dolls swiped: Evie's second-best baby doll, and Alice's white rabbit thing. The address of the little girls? Just wait for this. Oh, boy, but this just shows the way our luck is running! Ready?

Braddock Grove!

'Oh, what's the use?' sighs Wanda, looking as if *she* needs a shoulder to cry on.

'Like I said,' says Willie.

'What's got into you all?' says McGurk. 'We still have the rest of today and a half of tomorrow. And maybe these last two weren't snatched. Maybe they were just mislaid. Maybe—'

12.15 p.m. Another knock. Mrs McGurk this time. Very tight-lipped. No smile. Holding folded sheet of paper by one tiny corner.

'This,' she says, tossing it on to table, 'I have just found. In our letter-box!'

'This' turns out to be another note.

don't forget. Noon ToMoRRow "MISter Big" P.S. NOW it's Six doll S in DaNgER

12.45 p.m. I am eating my lunch. Fish fingers. My favourite, but I am not enjoying it. Then *my* Great Idea hits me. I have been thinking gloomily about the note and its cut-out letters, and suddenly – POW!

I jump up and shout 'Wow!' and nearly choke because I had forgotten I had a mouthful of fish finger.

Then I apologize and simmer down and bolt the rest of my lunch as quietly as I can manage and I excuse myself and I dash out of the house and I *run* all the way to McGurk's.

12

Black Thursday – Part Two

12.55 p.m. I track McGurk down to Turners' Sweet Shop. He is just coming out, talking to Ally Merrick and Marni Williams. They are now great friends in their trouble, holding hands and looking anxious. McGurk is crunching a sweet and telling them not to worry.

'And you'd better believe it, kids!' I cry. 'The case is nearly solved. Listen, McGurk . . .'

And I tell him then and there about *my* Great Idea.

Well, it is so good that he too gets all excited. He even gives me one of his sweets – which is very unusual.

'Ally,' he says, 'you may be seeing your daughter sooner than you think. Yours too, Marni.'

And to me he says:

'Right. Let's round up the others and organize the next move.'

1.30 p.m. In the office. We have now told Wanda and Willie about my Great Idea, which is this:

That Mister Big must have cut into a lot of newspapers and magazines to make his messages. So if we can find any cut-up papers in anyone's dustbin, we will have got him cold.

'And *now* we will see about those prime suspects,' says McGurk. 'Joey: you go look in the Pierce's dustbins. Willie: you look in the Camutys' bins. Wanda: you try in Freddie Leasor's. It's right next door to you and he was one of the rats who ambushed me. As for *me*,' he says, 'I'll take that creep Rafferty's.'

1.45 p.m. Outside the Pierces' garden. Mission accomplished. No trouble getting to look in the Pierces' bins. No luck either. Just goo. But I am not downhearted. Maybe one of the others has struck it rich. So I don't feel too bad about my idea. Yet.

1.50 p.m. Back in the office. Wanda there already. No luck for her, either. But there are still two good chances left.

1.55 p.m. McGurk is back, with sardine oil staining his sleeve. He is saying he never thought much of the idea anyway. But my fingers are still crossed. There is Willie yet to report.

2.00 p.m. Willie returns. Triumphant. Nose cocked high like a herald's trumpet.

'Look!' he says. 'It's not a newspaper or a magazine. But it has printing on and someone's cut a chunk off. So I guess that settles it. Tom Camuty is Mister Big!'

'And I am Mary Poppins,' says Wanda sadly.

And she is right.

Willie is waving a cereal packet.

We are shaking our heads.

'No?' says Willie.

'No, Willie,' I say. 'Tommy is not Mister Big.

Not on that evidence. All Tommy has done is cut out the label to send for This Month's Great Free Offer. See? It says it here. This month's—'

'Argh! Take the thing out of here!' snarls McGurk. 'It stinks!'

'Well it was a fair way down in the dustbin,' says Willie, lowering the soggy package.

'Out!' says McGurk.

2.05 p.m. Almost at once, after Willie goes out, we hear him yell.

'Hey! Fellers! Quick!'

'What *now*?' groans McGurk.

We go out.

We see Willie staring into the McGurks' dustbin, the lid in one hand, the cereal packet still in the other.

'Lu-look!' he stammers.

We look. We *stare*.

And: Wow!' I say.

And: '*Well!*' says Wanda.

And: 'How did *they* get there?!' yelps McGurk.

We are staring at a copy of the *Yorkshire Post*, folded in half, and a copy of *TIME* Magazine, not folded, just tossed on top. And we can tell it is those two, even though the yo has been cut out of the newspaper's title, and the ME out of TIME.

We soon see that other chunks have been snip-
ped out also.

Then we – Wanda, Willie, and I – we all turn
slowly and look hard at McGurk.

Very hard.

13

Mister McBig?

'Don't look at ME!' howled McGurk, out in the yard, next to the dustbin.

'Well it is your bin,' I said.

'And I wouldn't put it past you,' said Wanda.

'Heh! heh! Mister *Mc*Big!' said Willie, with a startling flash of wit. (It happens.)

'I – I've been *framed*!' yelled McGurk. 'Someone – somehow he must have got wind of your stinking idea, Rockwell! ... Right? ... Right? ... Hey, now! Fellers! Come *on*!'

Now he looked injured. His green eyes opened wide and stared straight into ours, one by one.

I don't know about the others, but I just had to blink.

'Sorry, McGurk,' I said. 'You're right. If it had been you, you wouldn't have made that condition. About admitting in public that the McGurk Organization is no good.'

'I should say not!' said McGurk.

'No, well...' mumbled Wanda.

'Su-sorry, McGurk,' stumbled Willie.

Then bang – immediately – McGurk went all clever again.

'I should think you ought to be sorry! All of you!' he said. 'And besides – call yourselves detectives? One glance should have told you.'

He was pointing at the printing.

'Huh?' said Willie.

'Yer!' said McGurk. 'Just one glance ... This, for instance. This YO out of the *Yorkshire Post*. You show me where Mister Big has used the letter Y in his notices.'

'In "Friday",' I said, quick as a flash.

Then I wished I hadn't.

McGurk leered.

'If you'd looked closely, dummy,' he said, 'you'd have seen he'd cut his FRIDAY out all in one word. Wanna bet?'

I shook my head.

'No,' he said. 'Because you'd lose ... Also another thing. This ME out of TIME ... Oh, yes! He uses a big M in Mister, and E's all over. But not—' he stabbed a finger at the magazine – 'in *colour*.'

He scowled round.

'Want to check? You still suspect me, any of you?'

We shook our heads and dipped our eyes.

'O.K., then.' And it really was O.K., you could

tell, because his face brightened. Very fierce, he looked still, but brightly fierce, and not at us. 'So Mister Big is *really* asking for it now. Trying to frame McGurk was *really* his big mistake.' He looked at us and became all businesslike. 'So put that lid back on there. And – hey! – throw that thing in first, Willie. It stinks. With a nose like yours you should be the first to—'

And that's when the Greatest Idea Of All arrived.

Just like that.

McGurk's again, of course. But I guess when a bloke's been nearly wickedly framed like that, he deserves to get such a dazzler. Maybe the shock does something to the brain, peps it up.

'Willie!' he cried. 'You're terrific, you know that? Ter*ri*fic!'

'Huh?' said Willie.

'And your nose is the terrific*est* thing about you,' said McGurk. 'Why – just tell me why – have we neglected you all this time?'

'Would you mind telling us what you're babbling about?' said Wanda.

'Yer!' said Willie, fingering his nose suspiciously.

McGurk looked all round the yard, eyes sharp and narrow. Then: 'Come back into the office,' he said. 'This is strictly Top Secret.'

14

Wanda's mission

It was so Top Secret – this plan of McGurk's – that I am going to have to keep it until the end. I am going to skip that meeting, when McGurk told us about it. I am even going to miss out how we worked on it to make it really foolproof.

I am just going to tell you what happened afterwards.

Well, first there was Wanda's mission. This was the bit that only she could do. Very important indeed. A key part.

And when I tell you about it, I want it to be as if you were watching from a great height. From up in a helicopter, say. And I have to do it this way so that you won't get too close to her. You will *see* what she is doing, but you won't get close enough for the secret to be given away.

All right then. If you had been up in a helicopter at about 4.30 that afternoon, you would have seen a very busy girl. You would have seen her run from McGurk's house and into her own house. You would have noticed that she spent about ten minutes in there.

Then if the helicopter wasn't *too* high, or maybe if you had powerful glasses, you would have seen what she came out of her house *with*.

In one hand: the list of neighbourhood dolls we made for that stupid census. (Now proving pretty useful after all.) And in the other hand: something bright yellow, and rolled up, but with one narrow end of it dangling, and – yes – you've got it – a tape measure.

Just an ordinary tape measure, to *look* at.

But really a *very special tape measure indeed*.

Then you would have seen Wanda go round to all the houses on that list, and talk to the girls who lived there. Or sometimes, of course, meet the girls outside in the street and talk to them there.

When she went indoors it would have been impossible for you to see what she did. Naturally. But sometimes, when the meeting was outside, you would be able to see.

Wanda was measuring the neighbourhood dolls.

Not all of them. Not all those little ones tucked away in odd corners, in dolls' beds, or dolls' houses, and such. Just the regular dolls in everyday use.

And why was she measuring them?

Well, that was part of the Top Secret. But her explanation was no secret.

'Just to complete our records, love,' she told each little girl.

And because they liked the idea of all this important measuring and recording in connection with their dolls, the little girls were glad to let her.

Now, because she only bothered with the regular dolls, she got through the mission fairly quickly. By 5.30 she was almost finished. In fact she had only one more doll to measure. One of her own.

Yes. This was part of the polishing up of the plan. This was one of those little extras that can make all the difference. This was a real smart move. It was one of those I suggested myself.

'Why don't you measure one of your own dolls?' I said.

She blushed and said she didn't play with dolls any more.

'Aw, come on!' I said. 'You must have one or two favourites stashed away somewhere.'

'Well, as a matter of fact, yes,' she said.

'So dust it off and bring it out,' I said.

'Yes!' said McGurk, catching on. 'Then – heh! heh! – give it the treatment.'

'You mean and then leave it lying around? In our garden?' Wanda was frowning. 'But he'll *suspect* it's a trap then.'

'No,' I said. 'Not in your garden. Lend it to Sue Gallon. Tell her it wants to visit her dolls. Only she mustn't take it in the house.'

And Wanda agreed, not looking quite so happy at the thought of using one of *her* dolls, but doing her duty just the same.

So although you wouldn't have seen Wanda measuring her doll, because she went back into her house to do it, I'm telling you about it anyway.

That completed the first part of our great plan: Wanda's mission.

The next thing we did was work out exactly what to put in the notice. McGurk, Willie, and I did this while Wanda was busy.

Then, when we all agreed it couldn't be improved, I typed the notice out, ready to tack on to the Griegs' tree first thing in the morning.

Friday morning.

.

79

15

The notice

We tacked it on to the tree at 9.00 a.m. exactly, that Friday morning. We took our time. We put it slap in the middle of the trunk, where everyone could see it. We even pretended to squabble about who should use the hammer and was it on

straight, and so on. This was done to attract attention.

But we needn't have worried.

This was the Big Day, remember. This was the day with the deadline. There was quite a crowd of kids even before McGurk hammered in the last tack. They all thought we were giving in already. Some of them seemed to like the idea. Vultures.

But no.

The notice wasn't an admission.

It was the opposite.

It was the loudest bit of bragging even McGurk had ever been known to blast out. And there it is, on the next page, just as I typed it.

'That should get him to act,' murmured McGurk, as we stood back and watched.

'It had better,' I said, suddenly feeling uneasy, thinking what fools we would look if 'Mister Big' *didn't* do anything between now and 11.00 a.m.

We had set a trap for him, you see. That was what Wanda's mission had been all about. But—

Well, we wouldn't know whether it had worked or not until the press conference itself.

And – believe me – that's what they mean when they talk about a 'nerve-racking' situation!

<u>IMPORTANT ANNOUNCEMENT</u>

The McGurk Organisation has done it again. We
said we would unmask "Mister Big" and so we will.
The case is now complete except for a few
details, and at <u>11.00 a.m. TODAY</u> the Head of the
McGurk Organisation -
J. McGurk
- will hold a PRESS CONFERENCE. All are welcome.
Be in the McGurks' back garden at 11.00 a.m. this
day, and you will hear his brilliant account of
how he and his brilliant team solved
THE MYSTERY OF THE KIDNAPPED DOLLS.
Also, he will answer those critics who say that
if it hadn't been for the McGurk Organisation
no dolls would have been snatched. On the contrary,
he will prove that only the McGurk Organisation
being alert and watchful has kept the total number
of victims down to 6. "Mister Big" just hasn't
been able to snatch any more. Nor will he. And why?
  "Mister Big" is doomed. "Mister Big" will be
unmasked. At 11.00 a.m. today.

Signed:

Wanda J. Grieg   *J. McGurk*

J. Rockwell

W. Sanders

16

The press conference

Just before 10.30 a.m. we had great news.

Wanda's doll had been snatched from the Gallons' front garden.

And at 10.45 a.m. came news of a second snatch. *Another* of the dolls that Wanda had measured!

'Oh, boy! Oh, boy!' cried McGurk.

It looked set.

The press conference looked like being a big success.

So now let me describe the scene.

By 10.59 a.m., all the kids in the neighbourhood must have been in McGurk's back garden. All kids under twelve, that is. And what made the garden seem even more crowded was that many of the little girls had brought their dolls along. Maybe they felt they'd be safer. Or maybe because the dolls had been victims, and their owners wanted them to see justice being done.

Anyway, with all those extra faces – doll faces, bear faces, rabbit faces, rag faces – that garden looked more crowded than ever. Really *weird* crowded – just like those old Dutch pictures Miss Jones showed us in school once.

The McGurk Organization stood apart. Naturally. We stood at the side of the house near the cellar door. McGurk had found some wooden boxes and we had put planks across them to make a platform. McGurk stood on an extra box in the middle, raised up like an Olympics champion. Wanda and I stood on his left, Willie on his right.

McGurk was wearing his best suit.

Well, at about one-half of a minute past 11.00 a.m., the critics got busy.

'O.K., it's time!'

'Who is it, McGurk?'

'Yer, McGurk! What you waiting for?'

'Let's hear it, McGurk!'

'Who is Mister Big?'

I was busy looking round, watching the faces. I felt like the Prime Minister's bodyguard. Looking for signs.

And I saw signs, all right.

Vulture signs.

Mainly the older ones. The Prime Suspects and their friends. Sandra Ennis and some of the 'secretaries' we'd turned down.

All kind of shining and tight. Waiting. Eager for us to fail.

I suppose it was then that I began to feel uneasy again. Maybe the idea was not so hot, after all. You get carried away. That's the trouble with McGurk's ideas. They *sound* good, and you get carried away with the preparations. Then: FER-LOPP!

I certainly hoped it wasn't going to be like that now.

Then McGurk spoke.

'First,' he said, 'a request. I want you all to keep an eye on one another.'

Heads turned this way and that: dolls' heads and kids' heads, quiet all at once.

'Why?' said a voice.

'Because if anyone tries to sneak off while I'm explaining, that one will be Mister Big.'

I felt uneasier than ever. Some of the critics were smirking again.

'Because believe me, kids,' continued McGurk, 'Mister Big is among us now. Right now. He won't have been able to keep away.'

McGurk sounded very cocky. He looked cocky. But I saw that behind his back his fingers were crossed.

I began to sweat.

'Anyway,' McGurk was saying, 'I told you we

would unmask Mister Big, and unmask him I will.'

'Get on with it then!' jeered Bert Rafferty.

'Yer!'

McGurk raised a hand.

'But first I have to admit *one* thing.'

Silence. McGurk admitting anything came as a shock.

'I admit I shouldn't have been so sure in the notice. About keeping the snatching down to six. Because since then there have been two more. Sorry,' he said, looking sad at Wanda. 'Sorry,' he said, looking at the other kid.

Acting, of course. All play-acting. I began to wish he wouldn't.

'Should think you *are* sorry!' jeered Sandra. 'Smart alec!'

More jeers. McGurk hung his head.

'And another thing,' cried Sandra. 'I don't believe he does know who Mister Big is. Do you?'

'Well ...' McGurk lifted his head. 'Well not exactly—'

'*See?*' yelled Sandra, all shining with triumph. 'I told you!'

'*But*,' said McGurk, 'in the next ten minutes I *will* know. And so will everyone else.'

That quietened the jeering.

'How?' asked Jerry Pierce, trying to sneer but looking pretty uncertain.

Now McGurk was smiling again.

'A trap,' he said. 'I made that boast on purpose. I wanted to make sure he *would* snatch a few more dolls. Especially dolls that Wanda had measured last night.'

'Measured?'

Sandra Ennis looked as if she couldn't believe her ears.

'What kind of a trap is *that*?' said someone else.

'Because,' said McGurk, with an *obnoxious* smirk now, 'because the tape measure was soaked in some very powerful perfume. Some her mother couldn't use. Scarum lilies.'

'*Arum* lilies,' said Wanda. 'So powerful I don't mind telling you I never want to—'

McGurk cut her short.

'So every doll that got measured got a nice helping of the stuff. And that includes the two that were kidnapped this morning.'

'Yes! Mine smells funny!'

'And mine.'

'Pretty perfume.'

A lot of the little girls were sniffing at the dolls they'd brought with them. I felt alarmed. We hadn't bargained for this. But McGurk was equal to it.

'Sure. Pretty perfume. And your fingers will smell of it, eh? Course! But you have a right to smell of it. They're your dolls. It's if any of the *fellers*' fingers smell of it . . .'

There was a movement in the crowd. All the boys were backing away from the little girls.

'Yes,' said McGurk, grimly but gleefully. 'That's right, fellers. Be careful. Because Mister Big's fingers are gonna give him away. Mister Big's fingers – heh! heh! – are going to *finger* him.'

'It'll be on them,' said Wanda, 'even if he's washed them since. Even if he's used *detergent*.'

'And that,' said McGurk, 'is where Willie comes in. Willie . . .'

Blushing but purposeful, Willie took a step forward.

'Willie has the most powerful smeller in this city. Maybe in the whole world. And Willie is gonna sniff your hands, boys, if you'll kindly line up along there.'

McGurk waved to the side of the garden. Willie stepped off the platform. The boys stood still.

'Of course,' said McGurk, 'if any of you doesn't want to let him sniff, that's O.K. *But we'll have a good idea why.*'

'Yes!' growled some of the girls.

'Oh, well!' said Bert Rafferty, with a shrug.

The boys began to shuffle into line, grinning sheepishly some of them, scowling some of them, but doing it.

Now I began to sweat harder. I mean this was *It*. I mean now it all depended on that nose of Willie's. And suddenly I remembered my attitude to it. How I had never been really convinced that Willie's nose was as good as he said it was.

I felt a pluck at my sleeve. It was Wanda. She must have guessed my feelings.

'It's O.K., Joey,' she said, looking none too calm herself. 'The stuff's so powerful even an *ordinary* nose could detect it.'

'I certainly hope so,' I said.

89

By now Willie was halfway along the line, stooping and sniffing. To his right, all the boys he'd sniffed were looking relieved, even laughing again. Of the Prime Suspects, Jerry Pierce and Tom Camuty were in the clear.

And on went Willie, clearing more. Stoop, sniff, O.K. Stoop, sniff – sniff again – white face of boy beginning to protest – O.K.

Now only three were left: Simon Courtney, Fatty Banks, and Bert Rafferty.

Even McGurk began to look worried as one sniff cleared Simon and two cleared Fatty Banks.

'Hey! Now don't all look at *me*!' cried Bert Rafferty in alarm. 'Come on, you! Get sniffing and clear my name!'

And he stuck his hands up and nearly wrapped them round Willie's nose.

Then we all watched – everyone: the Organization, the little girls, the dolls, the cleared boys, the girl critics – as Willie pulled a long face, screwing up his eyes, and backed off.

Whatever he'd smelled there must have been pretty powerful.

But it wasn't Arum Lilies.

No, sir.

That was the last of the boys and Willie was shaking his head!

'Mister Big'

Oh, the jeering! Oh, the crowing! Oh, the crying of some of the disappointed little girls!

'Hey! *Willie!*' cried McGurk, looking betrayed.

'Su-sorry, McGurk!' stammered Willie. 'But—'

Then Wanda got *her* idea.

God bless Wanda!

It must have been the extra agony of knowing *her* doll was in grave danger, too.

She grabbed McGurk's arm.

'Tell him,' she said in a whisper loud enough for me to hear, 'tell him to try the girls!'

'Huh?' grunted McGurk, looking dazed, shattered.

'The girls!' said Wanda. 'The older ones. Those who don't play with dolls any more. Just because the notes said *Mister* Big it doesn't mean it has to be a boy.' She looked round, her eyes gleaming. 'In fact tell him,' she cried, letting everybody hear, 'tell him to try *Sandra Ennis!*'

Sandra suddenly looked hunted. Right in the middle of jeering.

Already she was trying to shove her way through the crowd and out of the garden.

But I was on to her in a flash. I suppose I might have a try at being the Prime Minister's bodyguard when I grow up, at that. Quick reflexes.

'Oh no, you don't!' I said.

'Let me go!' she yelled.

'When you've let Willie sniff your hands!' said McGurk, taking charge again. (Quick recovery. *He* should think about being Prime Minister.)

'Why should I?'

'Why shouldn't you?' came the voice of Bert Rafferty. '*We* did.'

'Yeah, yeah!' came the boys' voices.

'Yeah, yeah!' came the little girls' voices.

'Mummy!' said one of the dolls, which was as good as a Yes.

'Well – well – all right then,' said Sandra. 'But – of *course* I'll have traces of the stuff. My mother uses the same perfume and – and—'

Here goes the case, I thought. Honestly, the way some girls can *fib*!

But Wanda was a girl, too.

Even as Willie was sniffing, and was then straightening up to say something to McGurk, Wanda stepped in and said:

'All right, kids! If *that's* going to be her story, why don't we go and check with her mother right now? And ask her at the same time to take a look round Sandra's bedroom.'

That did it. Mrs Ennis is a very *strict* lady. And if her daughter was caught telling fibs, let alone kidnapping dolls, it would be poor, *poor* Sandra.

'All right, all right! Please!' Sandra was trying to grin now. 'It was a game. A joke. That's all. Just—' she looked defiant again – 'just to – to show how poor this stupid detective organization is . . .'

But it sounded so foolish we didn't even bother to argue.

McGurk smiled. I'll say this: all he wants is to win, to come out on top. He's never bothered about getting the loser to crawl. I suppose he feels so tall himself at these times, he wouldn't be able to tell whether they were crawling or not, anyway.

'O.K., Sandra,' he said. 'Just fetch the dolls back here. They are unharmed, I hope?'

'I'll *kick* her!' little Ally Merrick was saying. 'Let go of me, Wanda!'

Sandra looked round and gulped.

'Of course! Of course they're unharmed. Like I said, it was just a joke and—'

'O.K. then. Fetch them back to their owners. Right now – er – *Miss Little.*'

I suppose it was a crack he just couldn't resist. Lucky for Sandra, too. The little girls thought that was a great joke. Some of them started chanting it, Ally included.

'Yes! Get going, *Miss Little*!'

Sandra looked mad. But it is better names than kicks, I always say.

And that was how we solved the mystery of the kidnapped dolls.

Later, of course, after the dolls had been brought back and everyone had drifted away, McGurk began to get odious.

'Brains, men,' he said, putting his feet up on the desk. 'That's what it takes, this job.'

'Yes,' said Wanda, 'and someone with sharp eyes to notice there are such people as girls around.'

'And someone with a sharp nose,' I said, feeling sorry for doubting Willie's, and wanting to make up for it.

Then Willie spoke. First time since out in the garden.

'Er – yes,' he said, and his eyes were lowered. 'I – er – was going to mention it out there, McGurk. You see . . . I nearly blew it.'

'What?' said McGurk, winking at us, feeling just fine. 'Your *nose* you nearly blew?'

'No,' said Willie, not even seeing the joke. 'Your plan, McGurk. Because – because just before Sandra Ennis, there was Bert Rafferty, right?'

'Right.'

'Well his hands – *phoo-wee!* – you should have smelled 'em. Onions! And I was still smelling them even when I got to Sandra, and – well . . . It was no *use*! I just wouldn't have been able to say whether she'd got traces of the perfume or not!'

Well!

Were we shocked!

But I reckon it was a good thing. It helped to cut McGurk down to size. Otherwise that bloke would have been unbearable for weeks. And far too cocky to handle the next case, which turned out to be the trickiest yet.